THE LITTLE GOLDEN
Uncle Wiggily

BY HOWARD R. GARIS

PICTURES BY MEL CRAWFORD

SIMON AND SCHUSTER   NEW YORK

THE LITTLE GOLDEN BOOKS ARE PREPARED UNDER THE SUPERVISION OF
MARY REED, Ph.D.
FORMERLY OF TEACHERS COLLEGE, COLUMBIA UNIVERSITY

ABOUT UNCLE WIGGILY

Uncle Wiggily, the jolly rabbit gentleman with the pink, twinkling nose, was born about 43 years ago, when he was created by Howard R. Garis. Since then he has been entertaining children in books and newspapers all over the world. This is his first appearance in a Little Golden Book.

THIS IS A BRAND-NEW BOOK
ILLUSTRATED ESPECIALLY FOR GOLDEN BOOKS

"NURSE JANE ought to like the bungalow much better after I paint it sky blue pink," said Uncle Wiggily as he stood on a ladder putting some dabs of color on his hollow stump house.

Uncle Wiggily had used up nearly all the color in one pot when he saw Billie Wagtail and Jackie and Peetie Bow Wow coming along.

"Hello, boys," called Uncle Wiggily. "Will one
of you please hand me up another pot of red paint?
My can is almost empty."

Billie the goat said he'd bring up some red paint, but instead, just for a joke, he took some green paint up the ladder to Uncle Wiggily.

"Won't he be surprised when he starts daubing green paint over where he put the red?" said Jackie to Peetie, in a naughty whisper.

"It will be a good joke," agreed Peetie. "But I hope he doesn't get mad at us."

Uncle Wiggily was so busy talking to Billie, Jackie and Peetie that he never noticed the color of the new paint. And before he knew it he had put some green color on the side of the bungalow where it ought to have been red.

The boys were so busy watching him, and then pointing out their joke to him, that none of them saw the skillery-scallery alligator creep over the crest of the hill.

"Oh, my," cried Uncle Wiggily, when Jackie and Peetie pointed out their joke to him. "Nurse Jane will not like this a bit!" Nurse Jane Fuzzy Wuzzy, as you know, is Uncle Wiggily's muskrat lady housekeeper.

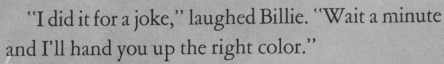

"I did it for a joke," laughed Billie. "Wait a minute and I'll hand you up the right color."

Nearer and nearer came the skillery-scallery alligator.

All of a sudden, as Billie was getting ready to take up the right pot of red paint, up rushed the funny old skillery-scallery alligator, with the double-jointed tail. He had been after Uncle Wiggily for a long time.

"Ah ha, Mr. Longears! At last I have you!" cried the 'gator. "Come down off that ladder until I nibble your ears."

Uncle Wiggily was so surprised that he spilled some paint on Jackie, Peetie and Billie. But still the bunny rabbit gentleman would not come down to have his ears nibbled.

"Well, if you won't come down nice and pretty when I tell you to, I'll make you tumble!" said the bad 'gator to Uncle Wiggily.

Then the unpleasant chap yanked the ladder out from the side of the hollow stump bungalow and the bunny rabbit gentleman began to fall.

"Oh, I am almost sure something is going to happen!" cried Uncle Wiggily.

The skillery-scallery alligator pulled the ladder so hard that it toppled into a tree near by. Uncle Wiggily gave a jump and landed on one of the branches. Billie and Jackie and Peetie held their breaths.

"Are you coming down out of that tree to let me
nibble your ears?" asked the snippy-snappy 'gator.
Uncle Wiggily said he would not.

"Then with my rough nutmeg-grater tail I'll saw down the tree and get you down anyhow," snarled the bad chap. So with his tail, which was just like a saw, he began to cut down the tree.

"Oh, we must save Uncle Wiggily!" whispered Billie the goat to the other two boys.

"Yes, but how can we?" asked Jackie.

"I know," barked Peetie. "We'll paint the alligator's tail red. Perhaps that will scare him away."

All of a sudden, when the alligator had the tree almost sawed through, and it was beginning to fall with Uncle Wiggily in it, the three animal boys rushed up with their pots of paint.

"Splatter him good!" barked Jackie and he and Peetie and Billie splashed different kinds of paint on the bad 'gator's back and tail.

"Oh, my goodness me!" grunted the skillery-scallery chap. "This will spoil my complexion! This is no place for me! I'll get Uncle Wiggily's ears some other time, I guess."

Jackie, Peetie and Billie splashed so much paint on the 'gator that the bad chap was glad enough to run away.

He looked like a broken piece of rainbow as he disappeared over the hill.

Uncle Wiggily easily got down out of the fallen tree, and he felt so happy, at saving his ears, that he danced a jig around the paint pots with the doggies and the goat.

"Well, I never!" exclaimed Nurse Jane, hearing the noise and coming out of the house. "This is a funny way to paint a house green, Uncle Wiggily."

But the bunny gentleman only laughed and continued his merry jig.